SOUP

SOUP

by

ROBERT NEWTON PECK

illustrated by Charles C. Gehm

A YEARLING BOOK

Published by
Bantam Doubleday Dell Books for Young Readers
a division of
Bantam Doubleday Dell Publishing Group, Inc.
1540 Broadway
New York, New York 10036

ISBN: 0-440-48186-4

Printed in the United States of America

Reprinted by arrangement with Alfred A. Knopf, Inc.

June 1979

30 29

OPM

Contents

SOUP

Chapter One

A Note from Miss Kelly

Dear Mrs. Peck,

Your son Robert made a rude remark to Miss Boland, our school nurse. Perhaps it was not intended to be as coarse as it sounded. Miss Boland thinks that you (his mother) should be informed of this. I quite agree.

Miss Kelly

I stood stock still in the kitchen while my mother read the note. Underneath my corduroy knickers, the underwear was starting to itch my legs. But I didn't scratch. Instead I just stood there and masterminded various routes of escape.

"What does the note say, Mama?"

This was step one. Soup and I had, of course, both read the note over and over all the way home and could have recited it upside-down in a barrel of water. But by asking Mama what it said, she would have to believe in my innocence. And as I asked the question, I made sure my eyes were open as wide and pure as I could force them. It was also a good trick not to blink as long as possible, which made your eyes water.

"Let me see it," said Aunt Carrie.

Aunt Carrie read the note, looked at Mama, and made her customary statement. It was what she always said, usually about ten times in just the forenoon.

"What he needs is a good, sound thrashing."

"Yes," said Mama, "he certainly does."

"No, I don't," I said. "It was all a mistake. Honest. It was really Miss Kelly's fault."

"Miss Kelly's fault?"

When either Mama or Aunt Carrie started asking instead of telling, I knew that the cause was not lost. There was still a chance to miss the whip, if I could just keep talking. And so I made the explanation as long-winded as possible to let their ire cool. Soup always said it was important to keep talking.

But I must advance with caution, being careful not to demean the noble name of Miss Kelly, who for the past one hundred years had taught first, second, third, and fourth grade (I was in third) in the small red brick Vermont schoolhouse. Kids who were my fellow classmates often remarked that *their* mothers and fathers had learned many a stern lesson from no other than Miss Kelly herself. So there was no way that I could push all the blame on such a worthy soul. I must step with stealth.

"Well," I said, "I don't really mean it was *all* Miss Kelly's fault. But the other day, she was teaching us on how to talk."

"A lesson you don't need," said Aunt Carrie, who believed that little boys and little girls should be seen and not heard—a rule that applied until our ages caught up to hers, which would be never.

"Miss Kelly said that when you talk to somebody it's like you're playing ball. First the somebody asks you a question, and that means they throw the ball to you. But you have to do more than just catch a question like you catch a ball. Here's the important part. You *have* to throw the ball back. When somebody asks how you are, you just can't say, 'Fine.' You say, 'Fine, thank you, and how are you?' "

"What does all this have to do with . . . ?"

"Everything," I said. "Miss Kelly said you have to throw the ball back. So I threw it back, and by mistake the ball hit Miss Boland."

Miss Boland, who was our school nurse, was about three times as big as Miss Kelly and about ten times as big as I was. You couldn't throw a ball anywhere in the whole world and not hit Miss Boland. That's when I got to thinking about it and almost giggled. Could have been a disaster, laughing when on trial.

"You hit Miss Boland?" said Mama. "I'm afraid, Robert, that I don't see all of this. Miss Kelly's note says you *said* something to Miss Boland. Did you?"

"Sort of."

"Exactly," said Aunt Carrie, adjusting her calico apron as if it were a judge's robe, "what *did* you say?"

"It's Miss Boland's job to be the school nurse," I said. "She comes around once a week to look at our teeth and see if we wash our hands. And she always looks in our hair to find cooties." (Nothing ever made Miss Boland happier than to discover wildlife in the thickets of some kid's hair.)

"Hmm," said Mama, "there's no lice in *your* hair." From that you could tell already that she wasn't too keen on Miss Boland.

Now was the time to start praising Miss Boland a bit to sound fair. I'd build up Miss Boland before I destroyed her, to heighten her fall. My one regret was that Soup wasn't here to enjoy my performance.

"Come to the point," said Aunt Carrie.

"She's a good nurse," I said. "She was just doing her job, that's all. It really wasn't Miss Boland's fault. She's supposed to ask me the question. She asks that awful question to every kid she sees."

"What question?"

"Did your bowels move today? And so I said, 'Yes, did yours?' I did what Miss Kelly said to do," I said, talking like a machine gun. "Miss Boland threw me the question ball, and I caught it and threw it back. That's the important part. So you really can't fault Miss Boland. She was only doing her job, like when she looks in my head for bugs. She's a good nurse. I just can't

blame Miss Boland for all of this. Honest, Mama, it's
not really her doing. If you're going to blame anybody,
you've got to blame Miss Kelly or me."

That ought to do it, I thought. Mentioning *my* name
and Miss Kelly's in the same breath would certainly
put me in the company of those who are beyond
suspicion. To punish me now would be like laying a
rod to Miss Kelly herself. No one in our town would
dare think of performing such a profanity. How could
a sane mind even entertain a yank down of Miss Kelly's
britches? They were probably made of iron.

"Did you apologize to Miss Boland?"

"Well, not right off. Because for a while I didn't see
how I'd said anything wrong. Honest. All I did was
throw back the ball, and I guess Miss Boland didn't
catch it. What made it worse was when the other kids
laughed."

"They *laughed*?" Aunt Carrie spoke in disbelief.

"Yes," I said. "Not all the children laughed. Soup
did and a few of the cut-ups. And that's what made it
worse."

"What do you mean . . . worse?"

"Miss Boland thought they were laughing at *her*."

"Were they?"

"No, they were laughing at me, I guess."

"What did Miss Kelly say?"

"Miss Kelly asked the class what was so funny. Nobody answered. So then Miss Boland went over and whispered in Miss Kelly's ear. All the while Miss Boland was whispering, Miss Kelly was looking right at me."

"And she never made you apologize to Miss Boland?"

"I did that before she told me to. Honest. But the kids were laughing, and I don't guess Miss Boland heard me say I was sorry. So you can't say this fuss is all Miss Boland's fault."

"No one said it was," said Aunt Carrie, "except you."

"It's not Miss Boland's fault at all," I said. "But I had to tell you the straight of it, so you'd understand why she does these things."

"What things?" said Mama.

"Looks in your hair for lice. She found a cootie in *my* hair once."

"She did not."

"Yes, she did. Honest. It was right after I'd been rassling with Rolly McGraw."

"Stories," said Aunt Carrie. "He's telling stories again. What he needs is a good, sound thrashing."

"He's just going through a stage," said Mama, "and it all started when he began to see so much of Soup."

"It's not Soup's fault either," I said. "If you have to blame somebody, I'm the one who made the mistake. Blame me."

"We shall." Aunt Carrie's voice rapped out like a gavel.

But I knew my confession would impress Mama, especially when I heaped the guilt of all the others upon my own little back, insisting that they not share the shame. I was right. My mother believed in me as solidly as I believed in her.

"Robert," she said, "were you rude to that nurse on purpose? Or were you only trying to do as Miss Kelly taught you all to do?"

There it was! A hole in the fence. The gaping gate to freedom. An escape from punishment and shame, not to mention pain. Even the way Mama said "that nurse" meant she wanted to believe that her good boy told the truth. All I had to do was say that I was just trying to follow Miss Kelly's sterling, character-building directive. But I couldn't.

"Well, I guess I knew it was wrong. But I can't stand it when Miss Boland asks that question. I didn't want to lie to her. So Soup and I figured it all out ahead of time. And I knew the other kids would laugh, because they knew I was going to say it. Soup and I drew straws. I lost. Mama, I guess you ought to whip me proper."

I got a licking.

I was lying upstairs on my bed, my eyes shut tight against the hurt. But I could tell by the sting of the whacks that Mama wasn't switching me very hard. Her head was even turned away like she hated the job.

She hit the wall a lot.

Chapter Two

Apples and Mrs. Stetson

SOUP WAS my best pal.

His real and righteous name was Luther Wesley Vinson, but nobody called him Luther. He didn't like it. I called him Luther just once, which prompted Soup to break me of a very bad habit before it really got formed. As soon as the swelling went out of my lip, I called him Soup instead of Thoop.

He first discouraged his mother of the practice of calling him Luther. (Using a different method, of course.) She used to call him home to mealtime by yelling, "Luther!" But he never answered to the name. He'd rather miss supper. When his mother got wise, she'd stand out on their back porch, cup her hands to her mouth, and yell, "Soup's on!"

From a distance (their farm was uproad next to ours) all you could hear was "Soup." And that was how the kids who were playing ball in the pasture started thinking his name was Soup, because he answered to it.

When it came to getting the two of us in trouble, Soup was a regular genius. He liked to whip apples. But that was nothing new. Every kid did. The apples had to be small and green and hard, about the size of a golf ball. The whip had to be about four to five foot long, with a point on the small end that you'd whittle sharp with your jackknife. You held the apple close to your chest with your left hand and pushed the pointed stick into the apple, but not so far as it'd come out the yonder side. No matter how careful you speared the apple, a few drops of juice would squirt on your shirt.

They dried to small, tiny brown spots that never even came out in the wash.

Sassafras made the best whips. You could swing a sassafras whip through the air so fast it would whistle. The apple would fly off, and you'd think it would never come down. To whip an apple was sport enough for most of us, but not for old Soup.

"Watch this," he said.

"What?" I said.

We were up in the apple orchard on a hillside that overlooked town. Below us was the Baptist church.

"I bet I can hit the Baptist church."

"You better not, Soup."

"Why not?"

"We'll really catch it."

"No we won't. And what's more, I bet this apple can hit the bell in the belltower and make it ring."

"Aw, it won't go that far."

"Oh, no?"

Soup whipped his apple, and I was right. It landed far short of the Baptist church.

"Watch me," I said. And with my next throw I almost hit the church roof.

"My turn," said Soup.

I'll have to admit that Soup put all he had into his next throw. The whip made a whistle that would've called a dead dog. That old apple took off like it'd been shot out of a gun, made a big arc through the sky, and for a few long seconds I thought we'd hear that old bell ring for sure.

But we never heard the sounding brass. What we heard was the tinkling cymbal of a broken window. Breaking a pane of plain old glass wasn't stylish enough for Soup. It had to be stained glass. Even the sound of that stained glass shattering had color in it. I just stood there looking at that tiny little black star of emptiness that was once a window pane. It was like somebody busted my heart.

"No," I said, in almost a whisper.

I wanted the glass to fly up into place again, like it never happened. So that the little black star would erase away like a bad dream. But there it was and there it stayed.

"No," said Soup.

My feet were stuck to the ground like I was standing in twin buckets of mortar. I couldn't run. Not even when a lady ran out of the side door of the church and pointed up at us. Even though she was far below, it felt like her finger took a stab right into my chest. It was a pain, just like when you get stuck with the tip of a sword.

To make matters worse, it was Mrs. Stetson.

My family wasn't Baptist. But I guess that she knew Mama and Aunt Carrie real well, because she came to call almost every week. Religion was her favorite subject. You'd be hard put to find a soul who knew more about God than Mrs. Stetson. She was a walking, talking Bible, which she could quote chapter and verse. Get her started and it went on like rain. Forty days and forty nights. Just to be in the same room with Mrs. Stetson was like being caught in a downpour. She sure could drench a body with scripture.

But what she was saying now was far from holy. And if there was anything Mrs. Stetson was poor at, it was talking as she climbed full-speed up a steep hill. By the time she reached me, she was so out of breath from the uphill scolding that she couldn't say a word.

I looked around for Soup, but he was gone. Good old Soup. So there I stood, with a sassafras stick in my hand and apple-juice spots on the front of my shirt.

Still wet. The mortar in my shoes had now hardened into stone. My ears were ringing with a *tinkle tinkle tinkle* of smashing glass that wouldn't seem to stop.

"You!" she said.

"Me?"

Her eyes burned with the wrath of the Old Testament. It was plain to behold that Mrs. Stetson believed that you had to smite transgressors so that the ground ran red with their blood until the multitudes were sore afraid. Especially sore. But if anybody ever looked sore, it was Mrs. Stetson.

"Robert Peck!" she said in full voice.

Her big old hands shot out and grabbed my face and my hair. She shook me hard enough to shake off one of my shoes. Then after she stopped shaking me, she twisted my head around so my nose was pointing right at the little black star of that broken window pane.

"Just look what you did!" said Mrs. Stetson. "Look me in the eye and tell the truth. Do you dare say you didn't?"

"I didn't."

This was not the response that she expected. I guess what she really sought was an outburst of guilt, a tear-soaked plea to ask for the forgiveness of God and Mrs. Stetson—perhaps not in that order of importance.

"I didn't. Honest, Mrs. Stetson. I didn't throw an apple that far. Look how far it is."

"You *did* do it. I saw you do it. And here's the apple you did it with." She had a pierced apple in one hand and my switch in the other, and I knew I was a goner.

"But I couldn't hit the church from way up here. Nobody could."

"Bosh! Even a fool knows how far an apple will pitch from a stick. Watch."

You won't believe what I saw. Mrs. Stetson somehow let go of her senses. She pushed an apple on a stick, and before I could grab her arm, her temper bested reason. Whissshh! You never saw a worse throw in your life, not if you stood up in that old orchard from now until Judgment. Her apple never even headed in the direction of the Baptist church. Nowhere near. But you couldn't say that apple didn't have any steam to it. No, sir. It flew off her stick (my stick) like a rifle ball, going east by northeast, and finally tipped over a flower pot with a geranium in it outside old Haskin's shack window. And the pot cracked the glass.

Crash-tinkle!

Out came old Mr. Haskin with blood in his eye. His language would have made Satan himself cover his ears. Not real fancy swearing, just a long string of old favorites. He pointed at Mrs. Stetson and me, then he started uphill and coming our way fast.

"Run!" yelled Mrs. Stetson. "That man's a degenerate."

We ran, Mrs. Stetson and I. She had on two shoes and I wore one, which evened the speed a bit, and we ran as if Hell was a step behind. We ran until we could no longer hear the terrible things that old Haskin shouted he would do to Mrs. Stetson the next time she came near his rotten old shack. We didn't stop running, Mrs. Stetson and I, until we darted into Frank Rooker's garage and had bolted the door.

But as we ran in, Soup ran out, after taking one look at Mrs. Stetson. Out the side door he shot, into the arms of Mr. Haskin. Soup still had his switch in hand, and his shirt-front was smelled and spotted with apple juice, which was enough evidence for old Haskin. Borrowing the sassafras switch, the old man gave Soup a fine smarting. I'll have to admit it sure must have been a sight to see.

Apples and Mrs. Stetson

From where Mrs. Stetson and I stood panting, we didn't see it. But we heard it all. Thinking I'd be next, I even winced for poor Soup with every blow. Best of all, we heard him confess up to breaking the window, even though it wasn't the same glass he got thrashed for. In a way, it really was justice.

Mrs. Stetson was right. There really is a God.

Chapter Three

Rope

I'LL SAY THIS for Soup. He almost always had some rope when rope was called for.

All it was was a gray length of rotten clothesline that his mother or mine no longer trusted to hoist and wave the family linens. But our rule was that we never *called* it clothesline.

It was rope.

We'd tie four or five feet of it on the end of a crooked old twig to make a whip. With a bit of luck, you'd snap it and make a crack of a sound, and some white cotton tufts would float into the air. Soup was pretty good at snapping other people, especially girls. Then he'd be the lion tamer and I'd be the lion. I never got to be the lion tamer too often.

If we had enough rope, we'd make a lasso. It was never called a lariat, always a lasso, and it was both noun and verb. You could lasso a kid with a lasso. But that was rare as accuracy. Everything and everyone usually got away free.

Soup's favorite pasttime was to tie somebody up. And this is how he always did it. He'd let me tie him up first, and then he'd turn free in no time at all.

But when Soup tied *me* up, I was usually tied up for most of the afternoon. And when he was sure I was securely a trussed-up captive, the torture began. These tortures were much too hideous to talk about, especially to those with faint hearts. The first torture was giving somebody who was tied up "a pink belly." This consisted of a few dozen gentle slaps where your shirt was pulled up. Unbearable. That was if the victim was tied to a tree. If there wasn't any rope (and there were four captors) the captive was spread-eagled in the air and dropped onto the ground several times from a height of up to six inches. This was called giving him "the bumps."

Or you could rub your knuckles in his hair real fast, and that was a Dutch Rub.

Soup's favorite torture was to give a "straw mouth." To do this, you take two heavily-seeded haystraws and cross them into an X. As soon as the victim bites down on the cross, you pull the straws, so that all the seeds come out in his mouth. Blood curdling!

Soup's worst idea was when he'd put a blindfold over your eyes. There was something about just not being able to see that made each torture more unbearable than it really was. Then you never knew what Soup was going to do to you. The fact that he never could think of anything very painful was beside the point. The blindfold was pain enough.

Another one of Soup's torture tests was an Indian Burn. This inhumanity was only possible if there was a length of rope left over, after the victim was bound to a tree, and two torturers. A small piece of rope was pulled back and forth across a naked arm or leg. Indian Burns usually produced little heat on the limb of the fortunate captive; but on a hot July day, the Indian usually worked up quite a lather. If there were two Indians, it also burned their hands as well, as there was little or no coordination when two Indians were yanking and counter-yanking.

Sooner or later I could always work free when Soup rode off to "rustle more cattle" and before he "returned to the hideout." But there was another kid who lived near us who was the meanest, bloodthirstiest redskin that ever held anybody captive. And *her* name was Janice Riker. She was the biggest and strongest and meanest kid that the world ever knew. She had a mop of thick, wiry, black hair and beady black eyes. She had the body of a hunchbacked, bowlegged ape and the brain power of a fully ripened bean.

Janice was a twelve-year-old giant at a time when most of us were nine or ten. At school, she was a year behind me and two years behind Soup. Miss Kelly was rarely impressed with her sums or her spelling. But as a mistress of torture, Janice was a real prodigy. When Janice Riker tied you to a tree, you knew you were tied for sure. Your hands went purple in ten seconds. Her knots were braided triumphs that took more rope than the loops around your body. And the one thing you'd have to say for Janice, she never forgot to put rope around your neck. Tight.

When the knots were all secure, Janice produced the dirtiest hanky in town, which was used as a blindfold if you were lucky; and if you were unlucky, as a gag. But seeing as Janice was such a perfectionist, she was usually willing to make a minor sacrifice for her torturous art. She'd kick off a shoe and use one of her smelly old stockings. Janice Riker sure had style.

If that wasn't enough, then came torture. Janice started things by stuffing a bug up your nose. The bug didn't go for the idea any more than the nose did and usually made its merciful escape. But by then Janice was just warming up to her trade. She'd yank down your britches and tell you she'd caught a hornet. That happened to me once. Only Janice wasn't faking. She really did have my britches down and she really did have an honest-to-goodness hornet. A real mad one! Janice let me see it, by lifting her stocking up over one of my eyes.

That was when Soup and Cubby came along.

Janice Riker was the only person in the world that Soup was afraid of, except for Miss Kelly, of course. But as for Soup's old dog Cubby, *he* wasn't afraid of the living or dead. Cubby was a mean one-eyed coonhound. Nights when the moon was full, you'd hear Cubby up on the ridge running after fur, and from a good mile off you'd hear him bugle. It was about the second most beautiful sound anybody ever heard.

The first came on the day that Cubby bit into the backside of Janice Riker and made her scream like it was murder. It was a holy note to my ears. Cubby never did take to me a whole lot. But he sure took to Janice, especially after she kicked him in the chops. Nobody with half a brain ever kicks a mean one-eyed coondog. I wouldn't kick Cubby if he'd been dead for three days.

But then Janice was about as smart as a bean.

And I wasn't much smarter the day I tied Aunt Carrie up. She let me do it, of course, thinking it was all a game and that she'd be able to turn loose right quick. She was willing. She put her back to one of those small tap maples in the little hollow west of our house, and she let me run around and around with my lasso. Aunt Carrie thought it was all a big joke, not realizing that I was a graduate of the Janice Riker Torture School.

"Okay," I said, "get loose, Aunt Carrie."

She wiggled and tugged, yanked and twisted. Then she asked me to cut her loose. I didn't. So then she ordered me to cut her loose. I still didn't. Aunt Carrie then promised me a present. I would get a "good sound thrashing" if she were not set free this instant. She would give it to me herself.

"How?" I asked her, laughing.

This was a mistake. I'd gone beyond the point of no return, and Aunt Carrie had a temper of a wet cat.

I began to wonder how I'd ever untie Aunt Carrie without getting thrashed. So I told her how sorry I was and that it was all in fun. To prove my good faith, I started working on the ropes. She quieted down some, and a bit of the red drained out of her cheeks. But it was a funny thing about those knots. I remember tying them as tight as I could. All of Aunt Carrie's struggling must have cinched them up even snugger. The knots seemed to be much smaller now. It was hard to tell where one loop locked into the next.

I was actually doing my best to untie the rope, but not fast enough for Aunt Carrie. She figured she was being put upon, so she started struggling again, which really didn't help loosen those knots that seemed to get more snug with each of her spasms.

CRASH!

It started to thunder. The skies were getting darker and darker as the knots seemed to shrink up tighter and tighter. Aunt Carrie started to panic. She was as scared of thunder storms as Janice was of Cubby. Even in the house, she'd cover her eyes with a dry cloth during an electric storm and put rubbers on her feet.

"Run to the house and get a kitchen knife," Aunt Carrie screamed at me, her little voice almost lost in the wind.

This I did. And the rain was really coming down so hard, I was soaked by the time I made it to the kitchen door. I got a knife (a dull one) and hurried out into the storm. The air was white with water, and the thunder was crashing down like Old Ned had a headache and there wasn't any Anacin.

"Good thing we're under a tree, Aunt Carrie," I said, as I sawed at the knots with little or no progress.

I was taking pains to destroy as little of my lasso as possible. Aunt Carrie had her eyes shut and was yelling bloody murder. She was now totally out of control. But somehow I heard her remark that during a thunder storm, under a tree was the worst place to be. A big bolt hit nearby, and Aunt Carrie charged like a stuck boar. The lasso snapped, and her hands were free. That's when she made a slight error. She started to run forward, forgetting that her ankles were still roped to the tree. Aunt Carrie landed face down in a somewhat muddy spot.

Whether I needed it or not, as soon as we got back to the house, Aunt Carrie gave me a good, sound thrashing. I tried to explain that if Janice Riker had held her captive, things would have been far worse.

It didn't do any good.

Chapter Four

Corn and Acorn

"MINE's GREEN," I said.

"The brown ones are better," said Soup.

"Who says?"

"Me, that's who."

"How come the brown acorns are better, Soup?"

"Look here and I'll show ya."

Taking the green acorn from my hand, before my fingers were quite ready to release it, Soup held it up next to his brown one. His acorn was rounder and fatter. The moon on my acorn was still green, the moon on his had mellowed to a rich, creamy, perfectly-rounded spot.

"See?" said Soup. "Brown acorns are ripe. And before it gets real dry, that's the best time to hollow it out for an acorn pipe."

Soup had his jackknife and I had mine. But my first error was clicking out the big blade, a natural mistake that was soon corrected as Soup pointed out that the *small* blade of a jackknife was special made to carve out acorns. Lucky for me our pockets were bumpy with spares, because I ruined the first three while Soup only spoiled one. At last the delicate surgery was performed. Under Soup's supervision, I even poked a tiny hole up from the point where the pipe stem would fit.

"Soup."

"Yeah?"

"What'll we use for a pipe stem?"

"Blue daisy."

"Honest?"

"Sure, but it can't be green. There ain't no hole up through the middle of the shaft unless it's brown and dry."

It was early October, the peak of the season for carving an acorn pipe according to Luther Wesley Vinson, the only available expert. Soup's theory did not concern the acorn. It was because blue daisy weeds bloomed at the start of September. But by October, the shafts were halfway green and partway brown; dry enough to be stiff and straight for a pipe stem, yet green enough to cut.

We located a weed patch that was laced with blue daisy that seemed, to Soup and to me, Created special to be stem material for acorn pipes. Each of us cut several stalks of the brownish-green shaft, average length, about three inches. With a bit of urging, one end could jam into the little hole near the point, the underside, of the hollowed-out acorn.

"Soup."

"Yeah?"

"We won't ever get any tobacco for our pipes."

"Don't need it."

"What'll we use?"

"Cornsilk," said Soup.

"Cornsilk? I heard tell that if you smoke cornsilk, your teeth turn yellow. And sometimes even your hair."

"Who said?"

"Rolly told me," I said.

"What would Rolly McGraw know about anything? He's so dumb I bet he goes to school on Saturday."

On any given day in Vermont, it doesn't take much brains to find a stand of corn. There was corn on our place and corn on Vinson's. I still don't know why we bothered to climb the fence into Mr. Tanner's, but we did. Some of the corn was late, and ears stuck out in pairs on almost every other stalk except the runts.

"Boy!" I said, stuffing handful after handful of wet green cornsilk into my pockets, "there's enough cornsilk here to smoke for the next hundred years. Maybe even a thousand. Look at it all, Soup."

"A million years at least," said Soup, whose experience in the fields of agriculture told him what a bumper season it was for cornsilk.

"Boy!" I said again.

"Let me see the silk you're picking."

"This," I said, showing Soup a handful that was long and green and wet.

"That'll never smoke," said Soup. "Don't you know *anything* about smoking? For something to burn it has to be dry. Ever see tobacco?"

"Sure. Lot of times."

"Well, what color is it?"

"Brown."

"What color is your cornsilk?"

"Green."

"Look at mine, Rob. I only pick the dark curly silk at the very end of the ear. Pick the stuff that feels so dry it'll almost crackle in your hand. See?"

"I see. Gee, Soup, you must know everything."

"Yeah, I reckon I do. At least about cornsilk."

It took me another five anxious minutes to void my pockets of wet green cornsilk. Some acorns fell out, and I saved those. My next harvest of smoking material was more selective, and I showed Soup some samples.

"How's this, Soup?"

"Well, okay. It could be better. Some of yours ought to be spread out on a rag under the kitchen stove for an all-night dry."

"What if Mama or Aunt Carrie finds it?"

"Then it'll smoke for sure. In the stove. And that old ass of yours will smoke too, if I got those two ladies sized up right."

"You sized 'em right," I said, remembering Aunt Carrie's apt description of a cigar: A flame in front and a fool in back.

"Rob, one of the things you got to learn . . ."

"What's that?"

"You ought to learn that if you're going to smoke, you got to do it in private. You can't spread out corn-silk all over the place for the whole doggone world to take note of. You can't run home and show people stuff that *you* like, but they won't even spit on. A while back I learned something."

"What?"

"I learned that my Ma and Pa weren't made to see everything or know about anything. So I don't talk about a thing. I wouldn't say *smoke* if I was on fire. One thing I just got to tell you, Rob."

"Okay, tell me."

"A shut mouth can bottle up a barrel of sin."

As we both sat and leaned our backs to Mr. Tanner's fence, we stuffed the bowls of our acorn pipes with dry cornsilk. It was pure joy to have Soup for a friend. A lot that Soup said made a heap of sense. He must of been part horse.

"See how I do it?" said Soup.

"Let me see."

"You have to pack just the right dose of silk into your acorn, or you won't get enough of a smoke."

"I know."

"But there's one mistake a pipe smoker can't make."

"What's that?"

"You can't punch the silk in too tight."

"Let's not call it silk, Soup. Say tobacco."

"Okay. You got to put air down in the bowl as well as tobacco. If there isn't any air, your pipe don't draw."

"Draw?"

"It won't let you suck any smoke into your lungs."

"Is that where it goes?"

"That's where."

Filling my acorn to the brim, with tinder and oxygen in full measure, I was now prepared. In my mouth, the blue daisy stem tasted bitter between my teeth. Someday, I thought, our pipes would be real, each briar bowl packed with a store-bought blend.

Soup struck a match!

As he put the flame to the open bowl of my acorn, my face puckered with the power of that first lung-filling puff, breathing in a subtle mixture of dry weeds, oak fruit, cornhusk, heat, and sulphur.

I had cut the stem a bit too short, and I had to look cross-eyed to watch the small crater that devoured the entire contents of my acorn in one raging drag.

"Inhale," said Soup, lighting his.

I inhaled. And in that one blissful moment of shock, I knew. As my entire soul converted from boy to blast furnace, active juices of my stomach (along with breakfast) surged upward to quench the fire that was now sweeping my respiratory and digestive systems. In all corners of my heart and soul (not to mention eyes, ears, nose, and throat) I really *knew*.

I was smoking.

Chapter Five

Cheating Mr. Diskin

"I DON'T THINK we ought to do it, Soup."

"We don't have to do it every time, Rob. But let's do it just this once."

"Well, I'm against it."

"How come you're against it all of a sudden? Didn't Ally Tidwell get away with it?"

"He said he did. Maybe he was lying."

"Ally don't lie," said Soup.

"Yes, he does."

"Name one."

"Well, he told me he caught a ten-pound catfish in Lake Champlain. And then a week after, his pa said it didn't even weigh six."

"Okay," said Soup, "so Ally fibbed about the catfish. Don't mean he lies all the time."

"I never said he did, Soup."

"Then why don't we try it once?"

"Just once?" I said.

"Just once, Rob."

"Okay, I'm game."

"I figure the whole trick is to find the right stone."

"Here's one," I said.

"Too small," said Soup. "That old pebble wouldn't weigh enough to make any difference. We got to get the price up to twenty cents at least, or it'll be one heck of a long trip into town for nothing."

"You're right," I said to Soup. "If our tin foil brings only eighteen cents, we both can't go to the picture show."

As we walked into town, Soup and I were silent for

a while. The very thought of missing the double feature was a Saturday afternoon tragedy. We both knew what was playing and had known for a week. The first movie was Stan Laurel and Oliver Hardy that had a gorilla and a piano in it. We'd seen the Previews of Coming Attractions on the Saturday before. The second feature was a cowboy movie with Dick Foran, the singing cowboy. Only in the movie he wasn't Dick Foran. He was a cowboy named Chip.

Neither Soup nor I could have missed seeing the double-bill of the day. To miss seeing those two shows would have been next to heartbreak. We just had to have twenty cents, as each ticket was a dime.

"We better hurry, Soup. We have to walk all the way to Mr. Diskin's and get our money and then all the way back to the movie theater."

"We need a stone," said Soup.

"It's wrong, Soup. Let's not do it."

"We could miss the show if we don't."

"You win. We'll do it. But I don't feel right about it, Soup. The only reason I'll go along is that we need twenty cents. Why in the heck didn't we ask Mama for a couple of pennies?"

"We should of," said Soup. "But it's too late now.

We're almost to Diskin's Junkyard."

"Almost."

"He's a Jew," said Soup.

"Who?"

"Old Mr. Diskin is. I heard somebody say so."

"Who told you?"

"I know who it was. It was the man who told Ally Tidwell that it was all right to put a stone in the middle of a ball of tinfoil and cheat old Diskin, because it wasn't really so bad to cheat a Jew."

"It's bad to cheat anybody. If we had twenty cents worth of tinfoil, Soup, I wouldn't do this."

"Neither would I. But I heard that guy say that there was no such thing as a good Jew."

"Maybe not," I said. "But if there was a good Jew, it sure would be Mr. Diskin. He's the only Jew I know, and he's been great to us."

"Yeah, he has," said Soup, letting out a sigh. "Hey! Here's a stone that's just the right size."

"How can you tell?"

"It's small, but it's heavy. Here. Heft it."

I hefted the pebble in my hand. It wasn't a very big stone, so I figured we really weren't cheating Mr. Diskin out of more than a penny or two.

"I'll do it," said Soup.

We unrolled our ball of tinfoil, planted the pebble inside at the very core, and wrapped layer upon layer of shiny tinfoil so it resumed its original appearance of a small cabbage.

Ten minutes later, Soup and I ran through the gate that was under the sign "Diskin's Junkyard." Mr. Diskin saw us coming and got up out of his rocking chair. He was smiling, just like he always did. Deep inside my stomach there was a small hard place, as if I had hid the stone inside my soul. I hated the whole business so bad I wanted to turn and run. But instead I handed the ball of tinfoil to Mr. Diskin. I noticed his hands as they took the ball from out of mine. His hands were old and white and seemed to be more like claws.

He put the ball of tinfoil on the old red scales that he weighed things on; and while the scales were balancing, he did his little trick—the one he always did. Pulling an old handkerchief from his pants pocket, he held it over his eyes. He pretended he was Justice, blindfolded with the scales. He always did it, and we always laughed. It was so absurd that it was funny, because it was Mr. Diskin's way of telling us that he was honest and that he gave everybody an equal price.

Soup and I both liked Mr. Diskin. We liked anyone who enjoyed a chuckle or two. He never talked. Mr. Diskin never said a word, just took your stuff and weighed it up on the balance, and then paid you the ten cents. Seems like he always knew that kids wanted a dime for the Saturday movies.

Soup and I held our breath. Mr. Diskin took our ball of tinfoil out of the balance and shuffled inside his old shack to get his money. That's where he kept his supply of dimes, but we didn't know exactly where. He must have had a thousand dimes back inside the darkness.

He was gone longer than usual. It seemed to Soup and me that he was inside for almost a year. Then he came out. But on this day he wasn't smiling. We held out our eager hands for the money. Inside my sneaker, my toes were moving around a lot. That was because I was looking at my feet. I didn't want to look at Mr. Diskin, and when I finally did look at his old face, he wasn't smiling.

Mr. Diskin handed us three things. Two dimes and a stone. It was the stone that Soup and I hid inside our ball of foil.

"Thank you, Mr. Diskin," said Soup.

"We're sorry about the stone," I said.

Looking at Mr. Diskin, I expected to see tears roll down his face or see him use his old hanky and wipe his cheeks. But he didn't cry. He just stood there looking at the little stone and moving his head back and forth a tiny bit as if his old hat was saying no.

On the way to the movies, Soup said, "I never felt as bad as I do right now in my whole life."

"Neither do I," I said. "I feel like a hunk of dirt."

"Me too," said Soup.

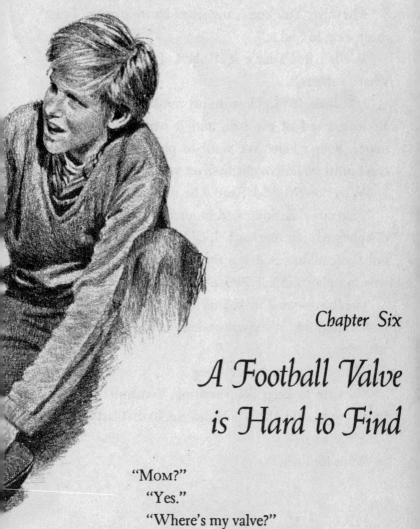

Chapter Six

A Football Valve is Hard to Find

"Mom?"

"Yes."

"Where's my valve?"

"Your what?"

"My valve. You know, my silver blow-up valve. I just can't seem to find it."

"Well, I don't have it. Robert, I don't even know what a valve is."

"It's silver. It's to blow up my football. Look. All the air leaked out of my ball, and it won't kick worth a hooey. Soup's here. We want to play football, but we can't until we find my little silver valve."

"Why don't you ask Soup if he has a valve?"

"I already did. Soup said he used to have one but it disappeared. His mother helped him look this morning, but she couldn't find it either. We *got* to find one or we can't play football. Please help look."

"Can't you see I'm baking biscuits? Whenever you lose something, it's always when my hands are white with flour."

"Hurry, Mom. Soup's waiting."

"I'd hate to keep Soup waiting. Someone as important as that. All right, where did you have it last?"

"Have what?"

"Your football."

"Soup's got that. But it needs air. What you have to find is my valve—please."

"Can't you blow up your football without a valve?"

"No. It's what you put the air in with."

"You used to have a football that had laces like a shoe. All you did was untie the laces and blow up the ball with your mouth through a little rubber stem."

"That kind is old-fashioned. The new kind blows up with a valve, but I guess you lost the valve."

"I didn't lose it. I've never even seen your valve. What color is it?"

"Silver."

"You mean it's the color of my good teapot?"

"Yes. Only it's little. It's only this long, about as long as my finger. It's like a needle."

"Did you look up in your room?"

"No."

"Then go look there, and I'll look downstairs. As I recall, you lost your valve before, didn't you?"

"Yes. But I found it in your sewing basket."

"Maybe that's where it is now."

"I already looked in the sewing basket, Mom. It's

gone. Maybe somebody just walked off with it."

"Who'd want one of those things?"

Mama was still talking, and I could hear from way up in my room. The valve was not under my bed nor in my chest of drawers. I looked up on my closet shelf. No valve. My throat was starting to tighten. Suppose we really couldn't find it and it really was lost. Or worse, some careless or unthinking person had stumbled on it and thrown it out. How could anyone do that?

"Is this it?"

My mother's voice rang out like a shiny beacon in a darkened world—a lighthouse upon desperation's lonely and rocky shoal. I almost broke both ankles jumping down the stairs. And there was Mama holding my silver football valve.

"You found it!"

"Yes, I found it. In the pocket of Aunt Carrie's apron. Robert, you are just going to have to take better care of your things. Learn to have a place for everything. That way you'll always know where your valve is."

"I will. Where's the pump?"

"Isn't it out in the shed?"

"Oh, I remember. Soup's got it. We were trying to

blow up the ball without a valve. It doesn't work."

Soup brought the pump into the kitchen from the back porch. We screwed the tiny barrel of silver into the threads of the pump hose. It was ready to be inserted into the football.

"You have to wet it first," said Soup.

"I know."

I put the pointed end of the valve (the one with the little air hole on the side) on my tongue and licked it several times. It tasted like silver. When somebody's mother blew up a football, she'd never wet the valve until we reminded her it was part of the ritual. And then she'd never lick it. Instead, she'd always wet the valve under the cold water tap. Mothers didn't seem to understand that the best part of finally finding your valve to blow up a football was to taste the silver. There is no taste in the world quite like it. It's the taste of an early morning in September, a Saturday when there's no school. The fields are still wet with morning, and some yellow leaves are already sprinkled on the pasture dew.

The taste of a silver football valve is all of that and more. It's the flavor of knowing that you had a pal like

Soup who was just as anxious to boot that old ball as you were. Neither one of us could kick it twenty feet, but that was of no matter. What mattered was that it was autumn, and Saturday.

Soup was holding the ball and I was working the pump with Mama helping. I was afraid we'd put too much air in and the football would explode. That's why Soup held the expanding ball. I stopped pumping.

"More," said Soup.

We gave a few more downward pushes in the old tire pump, and Soup yanked out the needle. The ball was perfect—swelled with air to the point that you could see the clean white part of the dirty threads along the seams.

"Let's go!" I yelled.

"Yowie!" said Soup.

"Not so fast," said Mama. "You left your valve in the pump."

"I'll get it later," I hollered over my shoulder as Soup and I headed for the open meadow of flat grass.

As we ran, we threw the ball back and forth, dropping it almost every time. It sure felt great to be alive on Saturday morning. Like the whole world knew it was Saturday and there was no school. It was cold and clear, and the sound of a badly kicked football punctured the air. The wind was as ripe as apples, so full of fall that you could almost bite every breath.

I could still taste the silver.

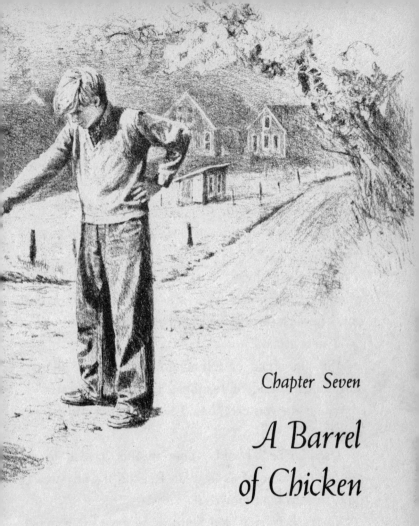

Chapter Seven

A Barrel of Chicken

"YOU'RE AFRAID," said Soup.

"No, I'm not."

"Then what are you just standing there for?"

"Well, it looks like kind of a steep hill. Maybe we should try it on the level."

"I knew you'd be scared."

"I ain't scared."

"Then why don't you get inside the barrel?"

"Here's why," I said, showing Soup a bent nail inside the old apple barrel.

"It's just an old nail."

"Yeah, but if it rips my sweater, my mother won't like it."

My mother already took notice that I look worse when I come home from school than when I start out. I never see a difference, but she always does.

"You're afraid."

"I'm not afraid of rolling down Dugan's Hill in a barrel. Just afraid of tearing a rip to the sweater."

"What do you care?" said Soup. "After all, it's *my* sweater."

"Used to be," I said. "Your mother gave it to my mother for some of us to wear. Reckon it's *my* sweater now, since you outgrowed it."

"That's because," said Soup as he gave me a punch on my arm for emphasis, "I'm bigger 'n you. I can't even get into that old sweater."

"And I can't get into that old barrel."

Soup looked around for a rock and found one. Rolling the barrel so the nail was against the ground, he pounded it flat against the raw, splintery wood.

"There," said Soup. "I fixed the nail."

With a doubtful eye, I got down on my hands and knees to inspect the barrel's newly-improved interior. I noticed then that some of the staves were rotten and loose.

"Get in," said Soup.

I started to back into the barrel, feet first, taking one last look down the full length of Dugan's Hill. I backed in only an inch or two, until I felt Soup's restraining hand tug on my belt.

"Head first," said Soup, "not feet first."

"How come?" I said, happily exiting on my hands and knees.

"Because," said Soup.

I knew better than to ask Soup "because what?" As far as Soup was concerned, his one-word explanation—because—was enough for me. It would be a waste of good time to offer further documentation for his decision that proper barrel-entering was performed head first. Argument would now be useless. Soup never made a moot point. And so with a sigh of resignation, Soup's sweater and I occupied the barrel in the approved manner.

The barrel, prior to my entry—or rather re-entry—

had been light inside. Now that I filled it, it seemed dark. To make matters worse, the inside bottom of the old apple barrel that I now faced still carried a few overripe remains of its recently emptied cargo.

"You see?" said Soup, "now when you roll inside the barrel, nothing can hit your face. There's a reason for everything."

I was about to add, "Nothing can hit my face except rotten apples." But I didn't. It would be folly to talk back to Luther Wesley Vinson when your arse end is pointed shoe-level in his direction and within his range, especially in such an undefended position. You had to know in this world when to keep your mouth shut and your behind inconspicuous.

"Ready?" said Soup.

"Ready." I really wasn't ready at all, not prepared in the least. But what good would it do to say I wasn't?

"Now," said Soup, turning the barrel with precision, "make sure you stay on the road. 'Cause if'n you don't, you'll roll off down the meadow and through a fence into Biscardi's hen coop."

"I will?"

"Not if you stay on the road," Soup said.

"How do I do that?"

A Barrel of Chicken

"Rob, don't you know anything about rolling in a barrel? Any jackass can do it."

"That's me," I said. "I'm in there somewhere."

"Remember this one thing," said Soup, his voice assuming his I-know-and-you-don't attitude, rather like Miss Kelly. No one ever questioned Miss Kelly. Her words were dipped in bronze.

"Remember to keep your weight even in the barrel. The important thing is balance," said Soup.

"Balance," I said in a hollow voice, as if it came from deep inside a barrel. It did.

"Brace yourself," said Soup. "And don't tear my sweater. I may want it back."

"No, you won't. It's got apple on it."

"You'll go on the count of three," said Soup.

"Why three?"

"That's the way you do it. As I holler out the number, you're supposed to say the same number. Okay? One!"

"One." I said.

"Two!"

"Two."

"THREE!"

On the final number, I never got a chance to answer.

Soup gave the barrel a heck of a push and also what sounded and felt like an extra kick, to insure I reached maximum rolling speed. Soup was a perfectionist in so many wondrous ways.

Down we went; the barrel, Soup's sweater, and I— down Dugan's Hill. I put fear out of my mind in order to concentrate on balance. Faster and faster the barrel rolled, so fast that some of it came apart. Around and around I went; my head was spinning, and I forgot what little I knew on the topic of balance. I did try to brace myself, but it didn't really matter anymore. When you walk *up* Dugan's Hill, you're not fully aware of its many and countless bumps. Yet rolling down it inside an apple barrel, each bump seems to make itself known.

Around and around, faster and faster and faster the barrel rolled. I figured there had to be *some* fun to it; and yet my mind seemed to be asking: when would the fun start? I tried to tell myself that it was great sport.

It didn't work. It wasn't fun. There was no joy to it at all. Not one bit. It hurt, it was scary, it made you so dizzy and weak that you wanted to cry, scream, and throw up all at the same time. And you got wood slivers in your hands.

Some people might call this fun. I sure don't.

A *Barrel of Chicken*

There was a loud noise, and then another. It sounded like a barrel with a fool in it, going at great speed, smashing through the side of Biscardi's chicken coop. I was thrown out of the barrel, but still moving, rolling, and sliding through a thick and slippery carpet of straw and hen manure. My last thought, as I slid into a hysterical group of Plymouth Rock matrons, as if they had been second base, was of Soup's sweater.

I'd have to be careful, I thought, as I tried to slow myself down by grabbing a chicken, or I'd really do more damage to the sweater than just a little old nail hole. Several staves out of the barrel and a rusty hoop seemed to be sliding along with me. It sure was a long hen house.

There was another crash, a chorus of excited cackles, and one very angry yell as I finally came to a stop just as Mrs. Biscardi dropped the eggs.

My first thought, as I lay on the floor of the chicken coop and looked up at Mrs. Biscardi with broken eggs dripping from all ten of her fingers, was that I hoped I didn't get any yellowy egg stuff on the sweater. Soup was a regular guy, but he could be right fussy about certain matters that concerned *his* property, both present and past. I put my hands on my chest to feel if the sweater was still in one piece.

All I felt was my shirt and part of an eggshell. To my dismay, I wasn't even wearing a sweater. And yet my arms were wearing a sweater and so was my neck. I was about to ask Mrs. Biscardi if she'd seen a brown wool sweater, but I decided she had other things on her mind. One thing that seemed to occupy her thoughts was a large, gaping hole in the side of her chicken coop. The hole itself wasn't so bad. The real problem was that most of the hens were running out through the hole and down the road.

I looked through the hole for Soup. No sign of him. Soup had evaporated as mysteriously as had most of his sweater. Mrs. Biscardi seemed to be even more emotional than even her most excited hen. There was at least a dozen hens flapping around and cackling their heads off. The air was a snow storm of chicken feathers, and so was the inside of my mouth. Mrs. Biscardi was saying things to either me or the escaping hens, and they didn't sound very friendly. But seeing neither the chickens nor I could understand even one word of Italian, none of us really took offense at the remarks that seemed to tumble from her lips without so much as a breath in between.

Mrs. Biscardi was dreadfully upset over something. She was so busy trying to guard the hole and trying to catch six or seven screaming chickens at once, while holding one hen firmly between her chubby knees, that it seemed to be an excellent time for me to scram. Getting to my feet, I ran out of the chicken-wire door. A piece of brown yarn was around my neck and I gave it a yank, but it didn't come loose. As I ran around to the other side of the hen coop, more yarn caught my eye. It was a long piece of yarn, starting from inside the hen house and stretching straight up Dugan's Hill.

I climbed the hill, following the strand of yarn as I retraced the route that I had rolled inside the apple barrel only a minute earlier. The yarn came to an end, snagged around a rotted barrel stave and wound around a nail.

It's not easy to believe how anyone could walk home smelling of rotten apple, broken egg, and chicken manure and be as happy as I was. I even whistled, despite the licking I'd probably get for the mess I'd turned myself into. But now I was a full-fledged member of that brave and fearless group of adventurers who had the courage to roll down Dugan's Hill in a barrel.

In my pocket was a large wad of brown yarn. So if Soup wanted his sweater back, I'd give it to him.

But he'd have to knit it all over again.

Chapter Eight

Hoedown with Chester Morris

"Soup?"

"Yeah."

"How come you do that to a bug bite?"

"I always do it."

"You make a X on each one?"

"Sure," said Soup. "See? I use my thumb nail and press a line into the bug bite that goes up and down. Then I press in a line that goes across."

"It's a funny thing to do."

"What's so funny about it? Cowboys brand their cows that way."

"No they don't."

"I just pretend that I own a big cattle ranch out west, and it's branding time whenever I see a bug bite. My ranch is going to be called the Itchy X. I'll name it after a bug bite."

"If I had a ranch," I said, "I'd put wings on an R and call it the Flying R. The R is for Robert."

"Or you could put the R lying down and call it the Lazy R."

"Speaking of lazy," I said to Soup, "you and me are supposed to hoe the potatoes. Your ma said she'd give a penny for every row we hoe."

"I did half my row," said Soup.

"Well, I guess I did about half of mine. That's half a penny for you and half for me. How will she ever pay us half a cent? She'll have to axe a penny in half."

"She probably won't pay us at all if she comes out," said Soup, "and sees us sitting here in the shade with our backs leaning against the toolshed."

"Maybe we ought to go back and hoe the potatoes, Soup. At least we ought to hoe one row, so we can each get a whole penny to our name."

"Rob?"

"Yeah."

"What you going to do with your penny?"

"Save it, I guess. How about yours?"

"I'm going to save mine too. And when I get enough pennies saved up, I'll go west and buy the Itchy X."

"Next year, I'll be saving up for an airplane," I said, "but right now I'm saving up for the goggles."

"What do you want an airplane for?"

"Maybe when I get my pennies all saved up, I'll buy an airplane and fly out west to visit you at the Itchy X Ranch."

"That'll be neat," said Soup. "You can come anytime. You can come every day you want to, after school."

"Then we can saddle up a couple of horses and ride the range."

"Just like Tom Mix," said Soup.

"I'll be Buck Jones. And I'll have a white horse called Silver."

"How ya going to get a horse on an airplane?" said Soup.

"Silver will be a trained horse, just like Buck's. All I'll have to do is whistle, and Silver will hear and climb inside the airplane."

"Horses don't do that."

"Mine will. I'll even have a big pair of goggles for Silver to wear over his eyes."

"What kind of an airplane you going to get, Rob?"

"Oh, I reckon I'll get a triplane. You know, the sort of plane that has three pairs of wings."

"Yeah, triplanes fly real good," said Soup.

"When I fly over your ranch, Soup, know what I'll do to say howdy?"

"Pee out the window."

Soup and I almost died when he said that. My stomach and ribs started to hurt, but I just couldn't stop laughing. Neither could Soup. We just rolled around in the tall grass on the north side of the toolshed, our arms around our bellies. It was several minutes after

Soup's sudden wit before I could talk enough to really explain how I'd fly over his ranch out west and signal a greeting.

"What I'll do as I fly over is dip my wings back and forth. That's what real airplane pilots do when they fly over people they know. I saw that in a movie."

"So did I," said Soup. "It was the Saturday you spit your gum out in the drinking fountain. The first movie had Chester Morris in it."

"Chester Morris sure is good in the movies. You know what, Soup?"

"No, what?"

"Lots of times I wished my hair was black and slicked down so I'd look like Chester Morris. I bet he takes a comb and parts his hair in the middle so it'll look real slick and shiny. So last night I tried to do it, too."

"You don't even own a comb," said Soup, "so how'd ya do it? Your hair is nothing but a lot of sandy curls. It sure beats me how you'd get your hair to look like Chester Morris when you don't own a haircomb."

"I used Mama's, and Aunt Carrie's good amber hairbrush."

"Did you soak plenty of water on your head?"

"Yeah, but it didn't help. What really made me try the whole business was when I found a bottle of Stay-Comb."

"Was there some of the stuff left?"

"Plenty," I said. "Maybe the guy who threw it away just got tired of looking like Chester Morris. So I put the Stay-Comb on *my* hair."

"Is there any left?" said Soup.

"No. I used it all. Must have been close to enough to fill up a tea cup."

"How'd it work?"

"Not too good without a comb," I said.

"Did you look like Chester Morris any?"

"Maybe a little. Not much. That old Stay-Comb sure is oily stuff. So I sneaked into my mother's room and borrowed her comb."

"Did your hair part in the middle?"

"No. The truth is, Soup, that comb of hers just couldn't part my hair at all, no matter how I twisted it."

"Did you comb it all forward first, so it's sort of down into your eyes. That's what my mother does sometimes. You're also supposed to stand very still."

"What does that have to do with hair?" I said.

"Beats me," said Soup. "All I know is, whenever my mother tries to comb my hair, all she ever says is stand still, stand still, stand still."

"Mothers sure are funny," I said.

"Yeah, but they do a lot of good," said Soup.

"My mother didn't do much good when she saw her comb."

"You didn't break it, did you?"

"No. All I did was wander into Aunt Carrie's room and borrow her good amber hairbrush. I guess I must have left some Stay-Comb on Mama's comb. At least I'd sort of wiped it off on my pants, but some of the Stay-Comb was left between all the teeth. Like white jelly."

"Never mind about that. Did the brush work?"

"It worked about as well as the comb," I said, "but I still was a long ways from looking much like Chester Morris."

"What happened then?" said Soup.

"Well, when Mama went to wash out her comb, Aunt Carrie came upstairs and asked me what I was doing with her good amber hairbrush. But after I told her, she put her hand on my head where all the Stay-Comb was. And then she pulled her hand away as if she'd touched something dirty. After that she took her hairbrush out of my hand and gave it a good look-at."

"I'll bet it had Stay-Comb on it," said Soup.

"All over it. Aunt Carrie asked me what I thought I was doing with her good amber hairbrush."

"What'd you tell her?"

"I said I was going to look like Chester Morris."

"What'd she say?"

"You won't believe it, Soup."

"Won't believe what?"

"Aunt Carrie looked me right in the eye and said, 'Who's Chester Morris?'"

"Some people," said Soup, "don't know anything."

"Well," I said, "maybe Aunt Carrie don't know who Chester Morris is. But she can sure handle a hairbrush."

"Did she brush your hair?" said Soup.

"Not exactly. She used the other side of the brush on the other side of me. And then she put my head under the pump."

"Wish I'd seen it," said Soup. "It's hard to picture your Aunt Carrie giving a spanking to Chester Morris."

"Gee, now that I still got some of that Stay-Comb on my head, do you really think I look a whole lot like Chester Morris?"

"Like you was twins," said Soup.

Chapter Nine

Eddy Tacker was a Bully

EDDY TACKER was so mean he'd pee on a puppy. I know, because he did it to mine.

Tam was just a tiny ball of collie when Eddy opened up his corduroys and did it. And that was something that even Soup wouldn't do. That was the difference between Soup and Eddy Tacker. Eddy was a bully; but not Soup, even though a number of his suggestions were made with convincing force.

As for Eddy, he made a hobby out of being mean. I hated him so much, I even knew his walk. For I could tell when he was coming up behind me with a dandy plan to jump on my back and ride my face into the mud. Or make me eat some.

To make matters worse, Eddy wasn't as tall as I was. Just a whole lot wider. I can't honestly say that Eddy was tougher than I was. But his best weapon was that I *thought* he was tougher. Of Eddy Tacker, I was scared skinny. Even in my dreams, he invaded peaceful settings and disrupted fantasy. He fed me to a dragon or threw me in a moat. But when I wasn't dreaming about Eddy Tacker, I was lying awake and thinking the sweetest thought a kid could ever think. *How I'd get even.* Little did I know how soon my next meeting with Eddy would be. Morning came. And with hardly a wink of sleep, I was fresh with deviltry.

It was the day after Eddy tinkled on Tam, and the air was ripe with revenge. I was upstairs in the schoolhouse balcony, and a boy named Carl Sprague was below. At the water bubbler I took a great gulp of cold water and let it loose, cascading toward Carl's head. But the water landed on Eddy. I laughed. Eddy did not. It wasn't the sort of thing that Eddy would take in the fun-loving spirit in which it was intended. Nor was it in Eddy's nature to pass it all off as an innocent accident and laugh the whole matter off. Not this Eddy. His only thought was punishment for the offender who wetted his dignity.

Eddy's one thought, as his wet, evil face looked up to the balcony was to avenge the wrong. But not a score-evening that was equal in severity to the offense. He would be dry in five minutes. Yet already forming in his face was a resolute promise to make me sting for a week. The worst part of Eddy's plan was to let me know in advance what my horror would be as soon as afternoon recess rolled around.

On the wall above Miss Kelly's desk, our schoolroom clock ticked slowly. Its pendulum was a great silver disk that swung to and fro inside its keyhole shaped case. Every tick of that clock brought Eddy closer. Miss Kelly finally rang the bell, a signal for us to line up two by two to be dismissed for the day. Behind me in line as we marched down the stairs, stepping on my heels as often as he could, was the bully himself. With each step he whispered his bloody intentions. Not loud enough for Miss Kelly's superb hearing to detect, but with enough carry to be picked up by surrounding classmates of both sexes, including Norma Jean Bissell. Several of my classmates tittered away as if the whole business of my drubbing by Eddy was one heck of a joke. A grapevine whisper took up the call, spreading the news of the afternoon's entertainment. All planned to watch, and probably even Norma Jean.

I didn't care if the other girls saw it. But why of all people would it have to be Norma Jean Bissell?

Norma Jean and I rarely spoke. What we shared together was a silent courtship. There wasn't even a carry-her-books-home-from-school arrangement, as we lived in opposite directions from the red brick building. Our only overt act of mutual recognition came once a day, as we sang "My Country 'Tis of Thee." As a class, we rose and stood by our seats, belting it out, stanza by stanza. All four. When we got to the line, "Thy name I love," I would look with longing at Norma Jean Bissell and she at me.

I thought of Norma Jean as my sweetheart, the girl to whom I would one day plight my troth. What she thought of me I never discovered, as we never exchanged words. Only glances. It was strictly a romance of song, like Jeanette MacDonald and Nelson Eddy.

But on this ill day, another Eddy was in the picture whose full intention it was to back me up against the schoolhouse and give me a whaling in front of Norma Jean and everybody. To make matters worse, Miss

Kelly picked this day of all days to keep Soup after school.

Out we marched, like a row of ducks. Two by two, all twenty of us. Down the slate walk, almost to the road. That was where I broke ranks and really turned it on. Never had I run so fast. Neither had Eddy Tacker, who was a step or two behind. His footsteps and his threats mounted in my ears. And that was when I saw Mama, waiting to drag me to the Dry Goods Store. My earlier distress had made me forget that she was meeting me to go to buy a new pair of knickers. My old ones had a rip at each knee. Boy, was she a welcome sight! Eddy, however, did not know the lady was my mother.

I got to Mama just as Eddy got to me. Turning to face him, I laced him in the chops with the hardest right ever thrown. Eddy crashed like a tree into me, and both of us into Mama. It was a mess. Almost all of us were crying. A hand had blood on it. So did one nose, and one dress. My knuckles were swelling up like a baseball glove, and so was Eddy's face. Five minutes later, the three of us sat in the Pharmacy and ate ice cream.

Eddy and I shook hands. I took note that he put a bit more pressure on my swollen hand than the sincerity of a handclasp demanded. Eddy went his swollen way home. Mama then snaked me to the Dry Goods Store. With his tape, old Mr. Cottingham, who spoke in fluent grunts, measured my girth and pointed to a pile of knickerbockers on a wooden table. He told me to take off the ones I wore. I was ready to balk at this, but one look at Mama said she had worked up a head of steam. So I thought it best to skin down.

The first pair of knickers was a perfect fit, and I said so. But Mama thought they looked a bit "pinched," whatever that is. Off they came. On went a bigger pair. And a scratchier pair. Too baggy. In those, I could be run down by a lame turtle. But helpful old Cottingham said I'd "grow into 'em." A third pair proved baggier and itchier than the second. I hated them and said so, and naturally Mama and Mr. Cottingham thought they were ideal.

Just to make sure my new knickerbockers were totally without fit or comfort, they had me climb up and stand on a table. They had me turn around so much, you'd think that's all I'd ever get to do—stand on a table and rotate.

Mama still wasn't satisfied. There were at least another six pairs in my size to try on. So she told me to take them off.

So I did. And I was standing on the table in my underthings while Mr. Cottingham jerked another sample of his baggiest burlap from the bottom of the pile. I looked over their heads and who did I see, coming into the store with her mother? Norma Jean Bissell, that's who. They both looked at me and I could have perished. Yanking the baggiest and scratchiest pair up over my hips, I announced how fine they fitted and how heavenly they felt. As they were several sizes too big, "to grow into," I couldn't feel a thing from my belt to my calf, where they buckled.

It was decided I was to wear my new knickers home. The old pair got wrapped, the new ones paid for. We started to leave the store, parading right between Mrs. Bissell and her daughter. Norma Jean pretended that she didn't see me. I pretended too.

We walked all the way home to our farm. It felt like I was wading through air. Every step, a pin stuck and restuck into my backside. But at least I was wearing my new knickers, and if I grew a lot every year and lived to be 103, they might finally fit.

But this was a small indignity. For on this day I could hardly wait to tell Soup how I had whacked Eddy Tacker and made him bleed.

Chapter Ten

Shoes

"HEY! I'M BACK," said Soup.

It was Saturday evening, and he'd been gone all day. But now he was standing at the kitchen door in his store clothes and his hair was still combed. Not actually so slicked as to have a part, but it wasn't all mussed up and curly like usual. For Soup, that was combed.

"How was it?" I said, as he came in.

"Great."

"Was it as big as they say?"

"Bigger," said Soup.

"Honest?"

"It's my guess that Burlington has got to be about the biggest place in the whole world."

"How many people did you see, Soup?"

"Oh," said Soup, leaning back in the kitchen chair and looking at the ceiling for guidance, "I must of seen a thousand or a million."

"Gosh, you must have been so busy saying hello to all those folks, you didn't have time to get new shoes."

"Oh, no?"

Soup unbuttoned his coat and took off his hat (the plaid one he always wore in winter with the red earlappers). Then he slowly unbuckled his left overshoe.

"Wait'll you see, Rob. They cost almost three dollars."

"Hurry up. I want to see 'em both."

Soup had a way of taking his time, especially if he

knew you wanted him to hurry. It was a trait of his nature that could drive those who waited half crazy. Everybody except Miss Kelly. There was a lady that you'd hardly list as one of your favorite friends. But give Miss Kelly this—she sure could handle Luther Vinson.

A day or so ago, she'd sent some of us up to the blackboard to do a sum. The rest of the kids merely erased the computations left by the previous scholar. But not Soup. He pulled out a wet rag from his pocket and *washed* his section of the blackboard until it was all black and shiny clean. He then had to let it dry. I wasn't up at the blackboard but in my seat where I could see Miss Kelly's foot under her desk. The way her foot was going tap-tap-tap, I knew that she was not as amused at Soup's standards of cleanliness as I was.

Miss Kelly kept Soup after school. She made him erase every square of the blackboard and dust the erasers. Then he had to wipe out the chalk tray; and on top of all that, wash every single square of blackboard all around the room. After that he had to empty the waste basket.

I'll say this much for Miss Kelly—she wasn't mean. Her role in life was not an easy one, with Soup and me around. So afterward, when the waste basket was empty, Miss Kelly told Soup what a good job he did. She said that she liked him a lot. Then she said that when she liked somebody, she called him Soup. But if she didn't like someone, he got called Luther *no matter who was listening!*

I know all this happened, as I was listening right outside the door. I'd sneaked back inside after we marched out, so I could watch Soup work or maybe get the ruler. But no such luck. There were no yelps of pain. Soup said "Goodnight, Miss Kelly." And she said "Goodnight, Soup. And you may wish the same to Robert."

Anyhow, getting back to Soup's trip to Burlington, this was what I was thinking about while Soup took his own sweet time to unbuckle both his overshoes. Then he put a toe on a heel and kicked off one, then the other.

"Wow!" I said. "Orange shoes."

"They're supposed to be tan," said Soup, "but I'm glad they look a bit orange."

"They sure do," I said.

"That's not all. Wait'll you hear the music they make."

"They make music?"

"Listen," said Soup.

He got up from the chair and walked around the kitchen. Every step he took in his new orange shoes made notes in sort of a squeaky melody. The left shoe played one tune and the right another. And when he stood stock-still on the floor and moved both, it sounded like some sort of an all-leather orchestra.

"It's like having birds between your toes," said Soup.

"Boy!" I said.

"The best part," said Soup, "is how you *buy* shoes like this. You get to look at your own feet down through an x-ray machine."

"What's an x-ray machine?"

"A machine that lets you look at your own bones."

"For real?"

"Honest," said Soup. "When you try on a new pair, the man at the shoe store takes you over to this machine. You climb up on a platform and put your feet into a little place inside the machine. Then you look down and see your own feet, and they're all green."

"Green?"

"Yeah. There's two other places lower down for the shoe man to look into and also one for your mother to look in. Then the shoe man points at the bones of your feet with a black pointing stick that's inside the x-ray machine."

"What's he do that for?"

"He does that while he tells your mother to see how much room your toes have to grow inside the shoes."

"What's it look like, Soup?"

"You can see all the bones of your toes. They look like a bunch of twigs. And when you wiggle your foot, the bones wiggle too."

Soup took a few more turns around the kitchen in his new orange footwear, making squeaky music with every step. It made me look down at my old shoes, which I'd had a long time. So long they hurt a bit to walk in. My feet were almost as big as Soup's.

We went upstairs to my room and fooled around with Tam, my dog. Then we played lotto, which was something like bingo, until my mother came in and told us how late it was getting. It was almost eight o'clock. So I got on my coat and boots and walked halfway home with Soup. At the halfway point, we said good night. It was real dark. Soup ran for his house and I ran for mine. We always did this for each other, whenever he came to my house or if I went to his.

On Sunday, the next day, we had a thaw. A real hot March day that chased away much of the snow. Above our farm, the hillside that faced south had big round spots of brown earth that got bigger as the day wore on until the meadow was a giant brown-and-white cheese. Holes all over. And all the gray rocks were bare and dry. They looked like sleeping sheep.

Monday morning was warm, too. Seeing as the road to town was dry and not muddy and the sky was clear, Soup and I got packed off to school in just our coats and hats. No mittens, no boots. I had my old shoes, and Soup sported his new orange pair.

"I'll race ya," I said.

We ran down the road. For a while, I was ahead of Soup. Looking back over my shoulder to see how close he was getting, I didn't see the root. It caught the toe of my shoe, and I turned around just as I pitched forward onto the still-frozen gravel of the dirt road. Both my hands were burning, as that's how I broke my fall. Just as Soup caught up to me, I turned my hands over to see all the gritty blood. Trying to get up, I saw that my right shoe was torn. It was damaged so badly that half the rotten old sole was flapping around like the mouth of an alligator we saw in a Tarzan movie. And

I could look down and see almost all of my red sock.

Maybe it was because I didn't outrun Soup or because my hands hurt too much to even wipe off the bloody dirt, I started to cry. And seeing Soup's new shoe—standing next to my old one that got all torn up—didn't help. I just sat there in the dirt and bawled.

"Hey," said Soup, squatting down beside me as I blubbered away, "don't cry. Don't cry, Rob. I got a clean hanky."

Soup dried off my eyes and cheeks. I tried to talk, but all that came out of my heaving chest was sob after sob.

I couldn't say anything. Soup was about as careful as he ever could have been as he blotted the blood off my hands. He didn't even rub. He just did it the way my mother would, as light as an angel.

"Why did you have to go and get new shoes, Soup? Why did ya?"

"Don't cry, Rob. Please don't cry. It wasn't my idea to get new shoes. My cousins just took me to Burlington."

"You always get everything," I said between sobs, covering my face with my burning hands. "I don't get nothing. I just get hurt."

"No, you don't," said Soup.

"Yes, I do. If we play baseball, you always get to be batter. And then when we're prize-fighters, I always wind up with the bloody lip." I was ashamed that I was crying so hard, but I just couldn't stop.

"Don't cry."

"I hate you, Soup. I don't want to go to school with you anymore, and I won't play with you anymore."

"Hey, Rob. What's the matter?"

"Look at my shoe. I'm going home. I can't go to school with this old shoe on my foot."

"Sure, you can."

"No, I can't. I can't. I can't."

Now I was really crying and couldn't quit. It was like somebody was shaking me all over, and I couldn't see or talk or even walk. It would have been all right with me to just lie there in the road forever.

"Well," said Soup, taking off his new orange shoes, "maybe you can't wear your old shoes to school, but I sure can."

Soup gave a good yank to the heel of both his shoes, and off they came. Then he took off my old ones and put them on his feet and put his new orange pair on me.

"Get up and walk," said Soup, "or we'll be late for

school. You know how Miss Kelly takes on when we're not on time."

"We're always on time, Soup. You and me, we're almost always the first ones there."

"Yeah," said Soup, "and we live farther uproad than just about anybody else."

"We better hurry," I said.

"How do you feel?"

"Okay. Your shoes are a little bit big for me. How do mine feel?"

"Well," said Soup, "one is awful tight, and one is awful loose."

"You didn't have to swap shoes with me, Soup."

"Maybe I just wanted to."

"Yes, but you were looking forward to wearing your new shoes to school and telling everybody about Burlington."

"I know. Hurry up, Rob. Why are you walking so careful?"

"So's I don't scrape your new shoes. I'd feel terrible if I knocked some of the orange off."

"I suppose the orange will come off sometime. Don't matter who does it."

"Gee, Soup. I can't believe it."

"Can't believe what?"

"I can't believe I really got your new shoes on my feet. Boy, are they ever big."

"Won't be long before I outgrow 'em, Rob. I'll even tell my mother ahead of time that they pinch my toe. While they're still orange."

"You will?"

"Sure I will, Rob. And as soon as I outgrow 'em, you know who gets 'em next."

"Me? You mean *me*, Soup?"

" 'Course I do. That's what pals are for."

"We're pals, Soup. I'll always be *your* pal."

I don't know how it happened. We were just about to go up the steps into the school, when I started to cry again. So we had to stop while Soup wiped my face into a smile. Then he looked me over to see if I was presentable enough to confront Miss Kelly.

"You look fine," said Soup. "Real fine. Your red socks go real good with my orange shoes."

"Thanks, Soup. Thanks a lot."

We ran into the schoolhouse and to our places. I felt like the whole world was looking at my feet. Miss Kelly noticed and smiled at me. And I was one of the very first that she sent up to write. All the way up to the blackboard, the shoes squeaked away like they were as happy as I was. I just felt orange all over.

Soup was right. It was just like having birds between your toes.

To the Reverend Luther Wesley Vinson,
a shepherd of his flock . . . from his first sheep.

R.N.P.
January, 1974